PONY PALS

The Last Pony Ride

Jeanne Betancourt

Illustrated by Richard Jones

A
LITTLE APPLE
PAPERBACK

SCHOLASTIC INC.

New York   Toronto   London   Auckland   Sydney
Mexico City   New Delhi   Hong Kong   Buenos Aires

No part of this publication may be reproduced in whole or in part, or stored in a retrieval system, or transmitted in any form or by any means, electronic, mechanical, photocopying, recording, or otherwise, without written permission of the publisher. For information regarding permission, write to Scholastic Inc., Attention: Permissions Department, 557 Broadway, New York, NY 10012.

ISBN 0-439-56005-5

12 11 10 9 8 7 6 5 4 3 2   4 5 6 7 8 9/0

Printed in the U.S.A.   40
First printing, January 2004

This last Pony Pal book is dedicated to Jean Feiwel. The Pony Pals began with her.

Thank you to my Pony Pal editors: Helen Perelman, Kate Egan, and Maria Barbo. Also a big thank-you to Elvia Gignoux. She was the equestrian consultant for forty-three Pony Pal books.

I have loved working with all of you. Like the Pony Pals, you made work fun.

Contents

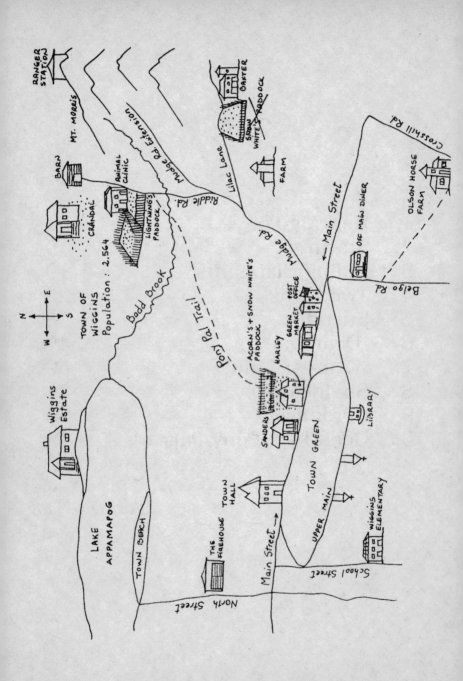

He's My Pony!

"Let's go, Snow White," Anna called out. She tapped the pony's sides with her heels and the pretty Welsh pony trotted smoothly along the trail. When they reached the end, Anna halted Snow White and waited for the other riders. Six-year-old Rosalie Lacey rode up on Anna's Shetland pony, Acorn. Pam Crandal followed on her pony, Lightning.

Acorn looked at Anna and whinnied as if to say, "Why aren't you riding me?"

"I'm sorry, Acorn," Anna told her pony.

"But I promised Lulu I'd ride Snow White while she's away."

"Acorn doesn't mind," said Rosalie. "He likes me."

"He isn't acting jealous or anything," added Pam. "Anyway, Lulu will be back in a few days. I can't wait to hear about her trip to Africa."

"Maybe she e-mailed us today," said Anna. "Let's go check."

"Can't we keep riding?" asked Rosalie.

"It's time to go to my house," Pam told her. "You can play with my sister and brother."

"Oh, goodie," exclaimed Rosalie.

Pam turned Lightning around to take the lead back along the trail.

Anna watched Rosalie move Acorn into line behind Lightning. She had to admit that Rosalie was a good rider. But Anna felt jealous seeing another girl on her pony. I'll be glad when Lulu comes home, she thought.

Pam was thinking about Lulu Sanders, too. Lulu's father was working in Botswana, Africa. Lulu had gone to visit him there for two weeks. Mr. Sanders was a naturalist who traveled all

over the world to study wild animals. Lulu's mother died when Lulu was little. For many years, Lulu traveled with her dad. But when she turned ten, he thought she should live in one place. That's when Lulu moved to Wiggins to live with her grandmother.

Pam remembered how Lulu found Snow White caught in barbed wire. Pam and Anna saw Lulu with the wounded pony and helped save Snow White. That's when the three pony lovers became the Pony Pals.

Now Anna, Pam, and Rosalie rode across the Crandals' field to the barn. The Crandal twins ran to meet them. Rosalie dismounted and went off to play with Jack and Jill.

"Let's tie the ponies to the hitching post," suggested Pam. "We can take off their tack after we check for e-mail from Lulu."

"Okay," agreed Anna.

Pam tied up Lightning and ran into the barn to turn on the computer. After Anna tied up the other two ponies, she leaned her head on Acorn's neck. "I love you, Acorn," she whispered.

"Hurry, Anna," Pam yelled from the office window. "There's an e-mail from Lulu. She sent pictures, too."

"I'll be right there," Anna told Acorn.

Anna ran to the barn office. She couldn't wait to read Lulu's e-mail.

To: Anna & Pam
From: Lulu
Subject: Hello from Africa

Hi, Pony Pals! Here I am in Africa.

Botswana is an exciting and beautiful country. ☺ This is where we are:

Dad and I went on safari with a man and woman who work with him. We saw so many animals. Rhinos, tigers, gazelles, zebras, wildebeests, elephants, and lots more. The elephants are HUGE and very, very smart. There are loads of them. The babies are cute. I like the way they hold their mother's tail with their trunks. I even rode an elephant at this animal preserve that my dad's friend runs.

The top of Dad's Jeep pops open into a tent. We can't have a tent on the ground because of the wild animals! We are in a city now. It's called Gaborone. I'm having a lot of fun. I wish you were here! I miss you. I miss Snow White. ☺ Give her a kiss and a carrot for me. See you next week. I got you presents!

Love, Your Pony Pal Lulu

P.S. Nobody rides horses where we are.

"Botswana sounds exciting," said Pam.

Anna nodded. "That elephant looked so big," she exclaimed.

"I miss Lulu," added Pam sadly.

"Me, too," agreed Anna. "I miss us being the Pony Pals."

Pam and Anna wrote Lulu an e-mail back. They told her what they'd been doing and how much they missed her. Pam moved the cursor to the SEND command and pressed the mouse.

"Let's have a welcome-home party for Lulu," said Anna. "Just the Pony Pals. I'll make a chocolate cake."

"Great idea," agreed Pam. "And I'll do a special mash for the ponies."

"We can make a big WELCOME HOME, LULU sign," added Anna. "You write the words, and I'll draw pictures."

Pam's mother walked into the office. Mrs. Crandal was a riding teacher and Pam's father was a veterinarian. So Pam had been around horses and ponies all her life.

"There are three restless ponies tied up

7

out there," Mrs. Crandal announced. "Is anyone taking care of them?"

"Oops," said Anna.

"We'll put them out in the paddock, Mom," added Pam.

Anna followed Pam out of the office. "I'm not going to put Acorn out right away," she said. "I want to ride him first."

Anna Harley had owned only one pony her whole life. And that pony was Acorn. First, she had leased the feisty Shetland pony. Then — when she was ten — her parents bought him for her.

Even before Anna had learned how to ride and had leased Acorn, she had loved ponies and horses. She was always drawing and painting them. Anna was a terrific artist. She wished that she could do art all day in school. But school was mostly reading, writing, and arithmetic. Anna was dyslexic, so keeping letters and numbers straight was difficult for her.

Someday I'll go away to art school, she

thought. Then I can draw and paint all day long. I hope I can bring my pony with me.

Anna mounted Acorn and rode him around the ring. When she moved him into a trot, she felt uncomfortable as she posted.

I didn't have trouble posting on Snow White, she thought. But Acorn and I haven't ridden in a ring in a long time. Maybe that's the problem.

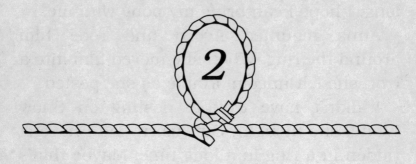

Starfire

While Anna rode, Pam sat on the fence watching Snow White and Lightning run around the paddock. Pam's mother was leading Daisy, one of the school ponies, out of the barn.

"Pam, could you come here for a minute?" Mrs. Crandal called out. "I have something to tell you."

Pam jumped off the fence. Her mother looked worried. Pam ran to her.

"What's wrong?" Pam asked.

"It's about Eleanor's horse," answered her mother. "Starfire."

Eleanor was an Olympic rider and Mrs. Crandal's best friend. Starfire was the most beautiful and wonderful horse Pam knew.

"You remember that Starfire strained a tendon last month," Mrs. Crandal continued.

Pam nodded. "You said he slipped in the mud."

"That's right," Mrs. Crandal said. "He's been resting in a stall for a couple of weeks now."

"Is he getting better?" asked Pam. "Will he be okay?"

"Yes," answered Mrs. Crandal. "But Eleanor won't be able to ride him in Olympic competitions anymore. She's already training a new horse."

"Will she ride Starfire at all?" asked Pam.

"No," said her mother sadly. "She has to spend all her time with the new horse." She put a hand on Pam's shoulder. "Eleanor has asked us to take care of Starfire. She

11

especially asked if you'd be able to ride him. He'll need a lot of exercise."

"Okay," agreed Pam.

"After a while, he can go back to jumping," continued Mrs. Crandal. "Not at the Olympic level. But you might be able to compete with him."

"I already have Lightning for jumping," said Pam.

"Maybe you're ready for a horse now," said her mother. "You've grown a lot this year. You're a tall girl."

"Lightning's a tall pony," Pam reminded her.

Her mother's next student — a redheaded girl — was walking toward the barn.

"My next lesson is here," Mrs. Crandal said. "Tell Anna I need the riding ring." Pam's mother led Daisy out to meet the girl.

As Pam walked toward the ring, she watched Anna riding Acorn. Anna usually rides better than that, she thought.

Tuesday morning, Anna made a chocolate cake for Lulu's welcome-home party. She called Pam while it was cooling. "I thought you'd already be here," Anna said. "We have to decorate the cake and make the sign. And don't forget the pony mash."

"I already made the mash," Pam told Anna. "And I'm on my way."

Pam was carrying Lightning's saddle out of the barn when a horse trailer came up the driveway. The driver honked softly three times and waved.

"Eleanor's here," Pam shouted.

Mrs. Crandal came running out of the barn.

"I thought she was coming tomorrow," Pam said.

"There was a change of plans late last night," explained her mother. "I forgot to tell you."

As Mrs. Crandal rushed down the driveway, Eleanor jumped out of the truck. The two friends met in a hug.

When Pam reached them, Eleanor hugged her, too. "Thank you for taking care of Starfire," she said. "I know he will be happy here." Her eyes filled with tears. "I thought Starfire and I would be a team forever. Now I'm training another horse."

Mrs. Crandal put an arm around Eleanor's shoulder and comforted her.

Pam went around the trailer and opened the side door. "Hi, Starfire," she said. "I'm going to take care of you."

The chestnut thoroughbred looked over his shoulder and whinnied a hello.

"That's some wonderful horse," said a man's voice. Pam looked up and saw her father. "Starfire and Eleanor were a great team," he continued. "It must be hard on her."

"It is," agreed Pam. "Can we take him out?"

"Of course," answered her father. "And I'll examine him." He unlatched the back of the trailer and backed Starfire out.

Pam, Mrs. Crandal, and Eleanor watched Dr. Crandal check out the prizewinning horse's legs. He gently felt the right leg. Then he felt the left. He looked over at Pam.

"Do you want to feel?" he asked.

Pam nodded. She loved it when her father taught her about veterinary medicine. She thought she might be a veterinarian some-day herself. She squatted next to her father and felt Starfire's lower legs.

"The right one is warmer than the left," Pam observed.

"It is," agreed Dr. Crandal. "Does the right one feel swollen?"

Pam felt again. "I don't think so."

"Me, either," he agreed. "That's a good sign."

When the examination was over, Eleanor patted Starfire's neck. "He's been cooped up in the trailer for three hours," she said. "I'll walk him around a little. Then I have to go back and ride my new horse." Eleanor stroked the white star marking on Starfire's forehead. "You'll always be my star," she said softly.

While Eleanor walked Starfire, Mrs. Crandal went back to the barn. It was time to saddle up the school ponies for a lesson.

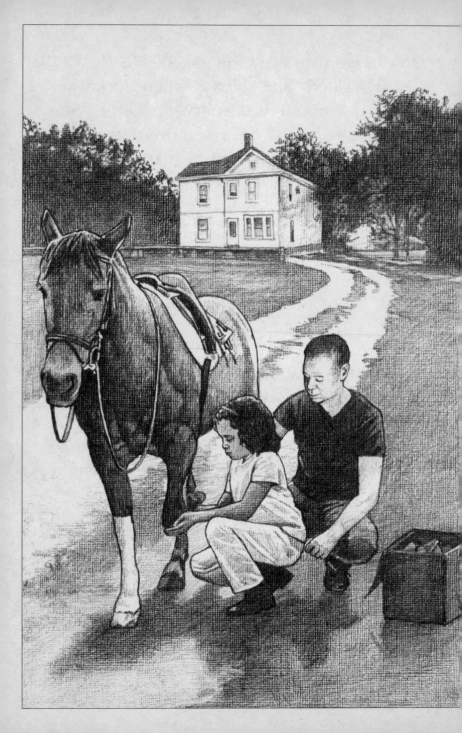

"How do we take care of Starfire?" Pam asked her father. "What do we have to do?"

"Come to my office," he answered, "and we'll discuss it."

Pam and her father talked about Starfire for a long time. She made a list of what she had to do for him.

HOW TO TAKE CARE OF STARFIRE — A TWO-WEEK SCHEDULE
   Regular diet
   Ride daily — walking, no trotting
      First week: 30 minutes
      Second week: 45 minutes
   Polo wraps on both Starfire's legs when riding
   Special groomings
   No vigorous exercise
   No rough play with ponies or other horses
   Turn out in small paddock
   Keep in stall at night
   Bandages on front legs at night

"The important thing," Dr. Crandal concluded, "is to not reinjure that leg. If you keep him safe and exercised, you'll be jumping him in a few months. Maybe Starfire will end up being your horse."

"I have Lightning," protested Pam. Thinking about Lightning reminded her of her Pony Pals. She stood up. "I was on my way to Anna's when Eleanor and Starfire came. Lulu's coming home today." Her head filled with Pony Pal thoughts. "Can we have a barn sleepover tonight, Dad?"

"Sure," he agreed.

"And can I go now?" she asked. "Will Starfire be okay?"

"Go ahead," he said. "Eleanor will want to settle him in the stall herself. You can start taking care of him later today."

Pam closed her notebook and ran out of the office. Lulu would be home any minute, and she hadn't helped Anna with the party. Would she be late for Lulu's welcome-home party?

Riding Elephants

Anna used frosting to draw a corral and three ponies on Lulu's welcome-home cake. She left space for Pam to write "Pony Pals 4-Ever." But where is Pam? Anna wondered. She said she was coming over right away.

Anna went to the yard. She'd already cleaned out the walk-in shed and groomed the ponies. An old sheet and painting supplies for the welcome-home banner were laid out on the picnic table. Anna painted a rainbow and flowers on it. Pam still wasn't there.

"Hi, Acorn," a cheerful girl's voice shouted.

Anna saw Rosalie and her brother, Mike, coming down the driveway. Rosalie ran to pet the ponies.

"Don't let them get dirty," Anna warned her.

"How come?" Rosalie shouted.

"Because Lulu's coming home in a little while," answered Anna. "I want Snow White to be clean."

Mike went over to the picnic table to look at the banner. Mike Lacey and his pal Tommy Rand were older boys who acted mean and liked to tease the Pony Pals. But Mike was a good big brother to Rosalie. He was only obnoxious when he was around Tommy.

"Is this something for Lulu?" Mike asked.

"Yeah," said Anna. "It's going to say 'Welcome home.' Pam was supposed to write it, but she's not here yet." She looked at her watch. "And Lulu will be here any minute."

"I'll write it for you," offered Mike. "I print good."

"Okay," agreed Anna. "Then maybe you can help me hang it on the shed."

Mike looked across the table at Anna. "How come Pam's late?" he asked.

"I don't know," answered Anna. "She's always on time." A cold feeling squeezed Anna's heart. What if Pam and Lightning had an accident on the trail?

I have to go find her immediately, she decided. But it will take time to saddle up Acorn. She noticed that Mike's mountain bike was leaning against the fence.

"Can I borrow your bike?" Anna asked. "I'm going to look for Pam."

"Sure," he answered. "Want me to write WELCOME HOME, LULU on the banner?"

"Okay," she answered. "Thanks." She was already on the bike.

As Anna cycled toward Pony Pal Trail, Acorn whinnied as if to say, "Hey, where you going?"

"Sorry, Acorn," Anna called over her shoulder. "I have to do something in a hurry."

Pony Pal Trail was a mile-and-a-half-long trail through the woods connecting the

21

Harley paddock with the Crandals' property. Anna didn't have to ride long before she met Pam and Lightning.

"How come you're on Mike's bike?" Pam asked.

"Are you okay?" Anna asked at the same time.

Pam told Anna about Starfire. "I'm sorry I'm late," she concluded. "But it was really important."

Lulu's party is important, too, thought Anna. "You should have called," she said. "I just hope Lulu isn't home already."

As Anna and Pam rode into the paddock, they saw Lulu getting out of her grandmother's car. "Quick, hold up the sign," Anna yelled to Mike and Rosalie.

Rosalie climbed up on the picnic table and Mike stood on the bench. They held up the WELCOME HOME, LULU banner.

Lulu ran toward her friends with opened arms. The Pony Pals met in a hug.

"Welcome home!" Anna and Pam shouted in unison.

22

Snow White cantered over to Lulu. Lulu hugged her pony, too.

She looked around at her friends and thought, I have big news to tell them. But a welcome-home party isn't the right time to tell it.

Two hours later, Mike and Rosalie were gone. Lulu's grandmother was back in her beauty parlor, cutting hair.

Pam and Anna picked up the party leftovers. Pam was already wearing the black T-shirt Lulu gave her. There was a herd of elephants walking around the front and back. Anna's T-shirt had giraffes on it.

Pam leaned over the picnic table and whispered to Anna, "Look at Lulu."

Anna glanced around the yard. Lulu was asleep in the hammock.

"She's jet-lagged," explained Pam.

With a finger, Anna swiped frosting from the edge of the cake plate. "When she wakes up, we can go for a trail ride," she said before licking it off.

"I can't," said Pam. "I have to go home and

take care of Starfire. Ride over when Lulu wakes up."

The first thing Lulu saw when she woke up was Anna. Anna was sitting on the ground drawing.

"What are you drawing?" Lulu asked groggily.

"You," answered Anna. She turned her pad around and showed Lulu the drawing.

Lulu looked around the yard. It was good to be back in Wiggins with her Pony Pals. Then she remembered she wasn't going to stay in Wiggins. Her father was going to be working in Botswana for two years, and he wanted her to live with him.

It had seemed like a good idea when she

was in Africa. But when she thought about telling Anna and Pam the news, she felt nervous and sad. I'll do it now, she decided. I have to tell them. She looked around the yard. "Where's Pam?" she asked.

"Pam had to take care of Starfire," explained Anna. "She said we should ride over there when you wake up. I'm so glad you're home."

"Me, too," agreed Lulu. She smiled, but she didn't feel happy.

Even when she was riding Snow White, Lulu didn't feel happy. She would be leaving her Pony Pals and her pony again. Only this time she was leaving for good.

A tear trickled down Lulu's cheek. She loved her father and wanted to live with him. And she loved being around the big animals in Africa, especially the elephants. But how could she leave her Pony Pals? How could she leave Snow White?

"It's so great to be Pony Pals again," Anna called over her shoulder.

It is, Lulu thought as she rode Snow White

over the familiar trail. I love being a Pony Pal.

The first thing the girls did at Pam's was to take care of their ponies. Then Pam took them to see Starfire in his stall. Pam was talking about Starfire as they headed to the house for dinner.

Lulu still hadn't told her Pony Pals that she was moving to Botswana. She had to tell them. Now was the time. Her heart pounded in her chest.

"I'm going back to Africa next week," she blurted out. "I'm going to live there. With my father."

"What?!" exclaimed Pam.

"Africa?" said Anna.

Lulu told them the whole story. How her father was going to write a book about elephants. That people spoke English in Botswana, and there was a school she could go to, and her dad had an apartment. She'd be going on camping trips with her dad, too. In the camping Jeep. She couldn't bring Snow White.

"You can't just leave," protested Anna. "We're the Pony Pals."

"But my dad — " said Lulu.

"Do you want to go?" asked Anna.

"No," said Lulu softly. "I want to stay here."

"Did you tell your dad you didn't want to move to Africa?" asked Pam.

Lulu shook her head. "It seemed like an okay idea when I was there," she said. "He's my dad. I missed him."

"He'll still come to see you sometimes," said Pam.

"And you can go visit him again," added Anna.

"I didn't think about that," admitted Lulu. She looked around at her friends. "I don't want to leave."

"This is a Pony Pal Problem," said Pam, "and we have to solve it."

Tears filled Anna's eyes. "We have to save the Pony Pals," she said. "And we will."

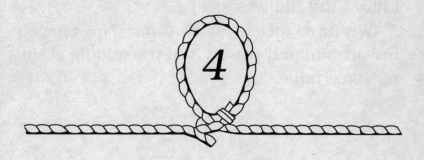

Two Ideas

That night, the girls slept in the barn hay-loft at Pam's house.

The next morning, Lulu woke to the smell of hot chocolate. She opened her eyes and looked around. Pam and Anna were already dressed and sitting at their hay bale table.

"Time for breakfast, sleepyhead," said Pam cheerfully.

"And a Pony Pal meeting," added Anna.

Lulu crawled out of her sleeping bag and joined her friends. They drank hot chocolate and ate raisin bran muffins.

"I don't have any ideas yet," admitted Lulu. "All I did was sleep."

"We have ideas," said Anna. She opened her art pad and placed it in the middle of the hay bale table.

"I don't get it," said Lulu. "What's your idea?"

"We need your grandmother on our side," explained Anna. "So she'll tell your dad to let you stay in Wiggins."

Grandmother Sanders had a beauty parlor in the front part of her house. She didn't like ponies or outdoor activities, but she loved fixing hair and doing nails.

Anna poured Lulu more hot chocolate from the thermos. "What does your grand-mother always want us to do?"

"Be girlie girls," answered Lulu.

"Right," agreed Anna. "And what would make your grandmother happier than any-thing else?"

"If we let her fix our hair," said Lulu.

"Exactly," said Anna. "We should ask her to help us do makeovers."

"Then, when she's cutting our hair," said Pam, "we'll tell her you want to stay in Wiggins."

"And ask her to talk to my dad," added Lulu. "That's a great idea, Anna." She turned to Pam. "What's your idea?"

Pam handed her notebook to Lulu. Lulu read Pam's idea out loud.

Lulu should e-mail her father and tell him she wants to stay in Wiggins. Anna and I will help her write the e-mail.

"Your dad doesn't even know you don't want to move," said Pam. "Maybe he'll just say yes."

"Especially if your grandmother is on our side," added Anna.

"Today's her day off," said Lulu. "Let's do the makeovers today."

After breakfast, Lulu phoned her grandmother.

"Makeovers!" Grandmother exclaimed. "What a lovely idea. I have a great idea for Anna's hair. A shade of pink nail polish would be perfect for girls your age. And there's a new aqua polish with sparkles."

"I bet Pam would like that one," said Lulu.

When Lulu finished the phone call, she grinned at her friends. "My grandmother can't wait to give us makeovers," she said. "She's waiting for us."

"I have to exercise Starfire first," Pam told them. "But you go ahead. I'll come over as soon as I finish."

"I told my grandmother you'd like aqua nail polish with sparkles," giggled Lulu.

Pam rolled her eyes.

"Maybe she can give you long fake nails,

Pam," teased Anna. "They'd be great for cleaning out stalls."

"My grandmother has a hairstyle she wants to try on you, Anna," Lulu added.

Anna clutched her long curly hair. "Oh, no," she moaned.

Pam put an arm around Anna's shoulder. "Don't worry," she said. "We won't let her cut it *all* off."

Anna and Lulu rode to Pony Pal Trail, and Pam went into the barn to take care of Starfire.

Pam talked to the beautiful horse as she cleaned out his stall. She told Starfire all about Lulu, Africa, and the makeovers.

Next, she took the bandages off his legs and groomed him. Pam loved rubbing Starfire's chestnut coat until it shone. He didn't move the whole time she worked on him.

"I'll take good care of you," Pam promised. "You're going to get stronger every day." Pam drew her hand along his smooth neck.

Her heart skipped a beat. She was the person responsible for Starfire now. She had to be very careful he didn't injure himself again.

Pam put polo wraps on his legs. Then she saddled him up and led him out of the barn.

When they were outside, Pam turned to Starfire. "Is it okay if I ride you?" she asked. She focused all of her attention on the big horse and waited for an answer. Starfire flicked his tail. Pam felt that he was ready. She led him into the ring, mounted, and asked him to walk.

As they walked slowly around the ring, Pam felt Starfire's power beneath her. She glanced toward the field. Lightning was grazing there with the school ponies.

Lightning is used to seeing me on other ponies and horses, thought Pam. I helped train Splash and Daisy for Mom. And sometimes I exercise the boarding horses. Lightning doesn't get jealous like he used to.

Thirty minutes went by quickly. "I could

have ridden you forever, Starfire," Pam whispered as she slid off the big horse.

She heard someone calling her name. Her sister, Jill, was crawling under the fence. "Lulu called you on the telephone," Jill said breathlessly. "She said you should bring a fancy outfit to her house. She said that you were going to have a new hairstyle and blue nail polish with sparkles. And guess what? Lulu's grandmother is taking you out to dinner."

"Thanks," said Pam. She'd been thinking so much about Starfire, she'd forgotten all about the makeovers. It was time to put Starfire back in his stall and saddle up Lightning. Pam wondered what Lulu's grandmother was doing to Lulu and Anna.

Anna looked at her reflection in the beauty parlor mirror. Her hair was straight for the first time in her life.

"I knew straight hair would look good on you, Anna," said Grandmother Sanders. She held up a bottle. "If you use this and blow-dry your hair every day, it can always look that good."

I like my hair curly, thought Anna. Besides, it's too much trouble to blow-dry it every day. But all she said to Mrs. Sanders was "Thank you."

Lulu's grandmother turned her attention to Lulu. "Now I am going to give you curls," she announced cheerfully.

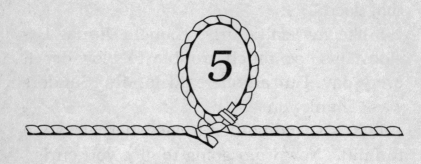

Surprise!

When Pam walked into the beauty parlor, Mrs. Sanders was giving Anna a manicure. Lulu was sitting under the hair dryer with a lot of curlers in her hair.

Lulu's grandmother smiled at her. "Pam, dear," she said, "I have some pink and silver beads to braid into your hair. Very feminine. Very pretty."

Pam wanted to protest. But she didn't. The Pony Pals needed Grandmother Sanders on Lulu's side. So they spent the rest of the day in the beauty parlor.

The part Pam liked best was learning how to give pedicures. Anna had extremely ticklish feet. Lulu had the second most ticklish feet. Pam's ticklish spot was under her arms, so she had a tickle-free pedicure. They put bright red nail polish on one another's toes. Anna painted little daisies on their big toenails.

Next came makeup.

"I'm just going to put on a little," Mrs. Sanders promised. But to Pam it seemed like a lot. She'd never worn eye shadow before.

At six o'clock, the girls went out to feed their ponies.

Acorn snorted and backed away from Anna.

"What's wrong, Acorn?" she asked.

"He doesn't like the smell of all that stuff in your hair," explained Pam.

Snow White came over to Lulu and nuzzled her arm.

"Snow White missed you so much, she doesn't care what you smell like," observed Anna.

Lightning sniffed Pam's head. She didn't mind the smell, either. But Pam backed away from her pony. "I'm afraid she'll eat the beads," she giggled.

Next, the three best friends went up to Lulu's bedroom and changed into their fancy outfits. When they were ready, they stood side by side in front of the mirror.

"We look sort of silly," commented Pam.

"We don't even look like us," added Anna.

Lulu agreed. She hated the curls in her hair even more than the gold-flecked pink nail polish on her fingernails.

"I hope we don't see anyone we know at the diner," said Pam.

"I hope your grandmother wants you to stay in Wiggins," said Anna.

"I hope all this is worth it," added Lulu.

On Saturday nights, the tables at the diner were set with light-yellow place mats and napkins. Each table had a vase with three yellow roses.

The Pony Pals exchanged a glance. They

were all thinking the same thing. They wanted to sit in the back where no one would see them.

"Can we sit in the back, Mrs. Sanders?" asked Anna.

"We love it in the back," said Lulu.

"We have a favorite booth," added Pam.

"We'll sit up front," announced Grandmother Sanders, "where everyone can see how lovely you girls look."

They sat at a round table near the front window and ordered sodas.

"Everyone unfold your napkins and put them on your laps," instructed Grandmother Sanders. She smiled at the girls. "This will be an excellent opportunity to teach you ladylike manners."

"Thank you for helping us with our makeovers," Pam told Mrs. Sanders as she spread the napkin on her lap.

"Lulu loves living with you," added Anna.

"I've enjoyed living with Lucinda, too," said Grandmother. "I'll miss her."

"Grandma, I want to stay in Wiggins with you," said Lulu. "I don't want to move to Botswana."

"Have you told your father that?" asked her grandmother.

Lulu shook her head. "I was thinking I'd send him an e-mail about it," she explained. "Do you want me to stay?"

Grandmother's face opened up in a big smile. "Of course I do. You are my darling granddaughter." She reached over and patted Lulu's hand. "There is so much I can teach you."

Anna covered her mouth to hide a laugh.

"Look who's here!" exclaimed Pam. "I didn't know Charlie was in town."

Mr. Olson and his nephew, Charlie, walked into the diner.

Mr. Olson owned a horse farm and was a friend of the Pony Pals. Twelve-year-old Charlie lived out west. He came to visit his uncle on school vacations. Charlie was a first-rate western rider. The Pony Pals all liked him.

Charlie and Mr. Olson saw the Pony Pals

and waved to them. The girls waved back. Mr. Olson sat at the counter, but Charlie headed toward their table.

"See why I wanted to sit up front?" Grandmother whispered to the girls. "All the young men will notice you."

Anna and Pam exchanged a horrified look. The makeovers! They'd forgotten. But Charlie didn't say anything about their new look. He just seemed glad to see them.

"We'll do lots of riding while I'm here," he said.

Just then, two more people the Pony Pals knew walked into the diner: Tommy Rand and Mike Lacey. When the boys saw Charlie, they came over to the girls' table.

Tommy took one look at the Pony Pals and burst out laughing. "Look at the Pony Pests," he shouted. "They're trying to be *girls*."

"Hey, quit it," said Charlie.

Mike looked at the floor and didn't say anything.

"Do your little ponies have dresses on, too?" teased Tommy.

43

"That will be quite enough, Mr. Lacey," said Grandmother Sanders.

Anna and Lulu exchanged a glance. Tommy didn't like being scolded by anyone — especially adults. They were afraid he would repeat what Grandmother Sanders said. He was always doing that to Anna.

Before Tommy could say anything rude, Charlie spoke up. "You guys want to hang out?" he asked Mike and Tommy. "We can walk around town or something."

"I can't," said Mike. "I've got to go home. We just came in for a soda."

"I thought you were coming over to my place to watch that horror movie," protested Tommy.

"I have to take care of Rosalie," Mike told him. "My mom's going to a meeting."

"Man, can't you do anything but baby-sit?" grumbled Tommy.

Charlie coughed. Anna could tell he was embarrassed for Mike.

"She's my sister," mumbled Mike.

Tommy left without saying good-bye to

anyone. Mike said good-bye and followed him out.

Lulu knew that Charlie liked Mike better than Tommy. Nobody really liked Tommy Rand. Except his mother and Mike Lacey.

"Why does Mike put up with him?" Charlie asked the Pony Pals.

"That's the question we're always asking," answered Anna.

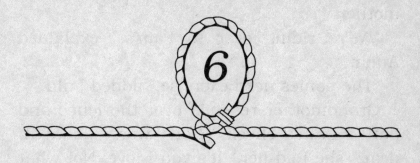

"Dear Dad"

When Anna and Lulu went out to the paddock the next morning, Acorn played his usual game of hard to catch. But Snow White ran straight over to Lulu.

"I never want to leave you," she murmured to her pony. "Ever."

While the girls were saddling their ponies, Lulu's grandmother came outside.

"Riding helmets will crush your new hairdos," Grandmother Sanders said.

Lulu led Snow White to the fence. "I'm sorry I'm going to mess up my hair after you curled it and everything," she told her grand-mother.

"We're riding over to Pam's," explained Anna.

"The ponies need exercise," added Lulu.

Grandmother reached over the fence and patted Lulu's cheek. "Don't worry about it, dear," she told her. "It's you I love. Not what your hair looks like. You girls ride safely. Okay?"

"Okay," they agreed in unison.

As Lulu rode onto Pony Pal Trail, she thought about her grandmother. Even though they liked different things, Lulu loved her a lot. If her dad made her leave Wiggins, she would miss Grandmother Sanders.

At the other end of the trail, Pam was grooming Starfire. She put on his polo wraps, saddled him up, and led him to the riding ring. Pam loved being on the big, smooth-riding horse. When they came out of the second turn, she saw her mother at the gate.

Pam rode over to her. "Do you need the ring for a lesson, Mom?" she asked.

"No," answered her mother. "But I'd like to use Lightning for a lesson at nine-thirty. She's the best jumping pony we've got."

"Okay," agreed Pam. "But after that, I'm taking her for a trail ride with Anna and Lulu."

"In a few weeks you can start using Starfire for trail rides," said her mother.

"I have Lightning for trail rides, Mom," Pam reminded her. "Besides, when Starfire's better, Eleanor will take him back."

Mrs. Crandal reached over the gate and patted Starfire's neck. She grinned at Pam. "Haven't you guessed yet?" she said.

"Guessed what?" asked Pam.

"Eleanor is giving Starfire to you, honey," she answered. "He'll be your horse. He is already."

"He is!" exclaimed Pam. Ideas tumbled through her head and a rush of words poured out of her. "Starfire is Eleanor's horse. . . . Doesn't she love him anymore? . . .

I'm not ready for a horse. . . . I still ride Lightning really well. . . . Lightning is my pony. . . . I'm a *Pony* Pal. . . ."

Mrs. Crandal put up her hand. "Whoa," she said. "Why don't we talk about this when you've finished exercising your horse?" Pam's mother turned and walked away.

Pam was left alone in the ring with Starfire.

Tears filled her eyes. They were tears of joy and tears of sadness.

She felt the big, calm horse beneath her. They'd been halted for a while. She had gotten very excited. But Starfire hadn't moved a muscle or made a sound. Pam put her hand on his neck and focused on him. She understood that Starfire was waiting for her. He was ready to do whatever she wanted. Pam touched her heels lightly to the powerful horse's side and he moved forward.

Pam was leading Starfire out of the ring when she saw Anna and Lulu riding toward her. I'm not going to tell them that

Eleanor gave me Starfire, she thought. Not yet.

Anna and Lulu put their ponies in the paddock with Lightning and the school ponies. Then they went to the new barn where Pam was putting Starfire in his stall.

"He's so beautiful," said Anna.

"Eleanor must miss him," added Lulu.

Pam kissed Starfire's white star marking. My horse, she thought. Starfire is my horse.

"Doesn't Lightning get jealous because you're taking care of Starfire?" asked Anna.

"Lightning's busy," answered Pam. "She's helping my mother with lessons."

Anna and Lulu exchanged a glance. They were both thinking the same thing. Pam used to worry about Lightning being jealous.

"Can we write the e-mail now?" asked Anna.

A few minutes later, the girls sat around the computer in the barn office and went online.

51

They worked on the letter until they agreed that it was perfect.

To: Dad
From: Lulu
Subject: Here I am in Wiggins

Dear Dad,
Pam and Anna had a party for me when I came home. I was so happy to see them and Snow White. ☺ Anna said that Snow White missed me. Snow White always comes right to me when I go out to the paddock now. There is no better pony in the world for me. I loved riding the elephant, Dad. I never thought I would do something like that. It was exciting. I liked the whole safari. Seeing all those animals was also very exciting. You are lucky to live in such an interesting place.
But I've been thinking about something, Dad. I don't want to live in Botswana like you do. I want to stay in Wiggins. There are many reasons for my decision. Here are some of them:

1. I would miss Grandma.
2. Grandma wants me to stay with her.
3. I don't want to stop being a Pony Pal.
4. Wiggins feels like my home now.
5. I don't want to leave Snow White. I can't imagine my life without her.

I will visit you in Africa, Dad. You'll come visit, too.

I love you very much, Dad. And I miss you.

But, please, may I stay in Wiggins?

XXX OOO

Your daughter,

Lulu

P.S. Anna and Pam say hi. So does Snow White.

"Ready. Set. Go," said Pam. She pressed the mouse. "The e-mail is on its way to your dad, Lulu."

Anna held up her crossed fingers. "I hope it works," she said. "I hope it with all my heart."

Pam and Lulu crossed their fingers. "Me, too," they said in unison.

* * *

While Lightning finished the jumping lesson, the Pony Pals packed a picnic lunch.

An hour later, they were riding on Ms. Wiggins's trails. Ms. Wiggins was a friend of the Pony Pals and had wonderful trails through the woods. They could ride on her property whenever they wanted.

As Anna rode, she shifted uncomfortably in the saddle. Acorn's my pony, she thought. Why can't I ride him as well as I ride Snow White?

Pam was thinking about how she was riding, too. My mother's right, she thought. I'm pulling my legs up when I ride. I *am* getting too tall for Lightning. She looked ahead at Anna and thought, Anna's outgrowing Acorn, too.

As Lulu rode, she wished that she could live in two places at once. If I stay in Wiggins, she thought, how long will it be until I see my dad again? Then a new thought popped into her head. Will Dad think that I don't love him if I don't want to move?

When the riders reached their favorite spot on Badd Brook, they stopped. The ponies drank from the brook while the girls picnicked.

"I have some big news," announced Pam.

"What?" asked Lulu. "Is it good news?"

"It's really great news," answered Pam. She looked over at the three ponies. Lightning raised her head. The sunlight lit up her upside-down heart marking. Pam's heart ached. She was too big for her pony. "And it's sad news," she added.

"Something that is great news and sad news at the same time," said Anna. "That sounds like a riddle. Is it a joke?"

"No," said Pam seriously, "it isn't."

Lulu dipped her hand in the cool brook water. "Tell us the sad part first," she said.

"The sad part is that I've outgrown Lightning," said Pam. She looked at Anna. "I think you're too big for Acorn, too. That's why you haven't been riding as well as you used to. I watched you. You keep raising your legs."

"That's a dumb thing to say," said Anna. "I'm shorter than you."

"We're all growing," explained Pam. "And our ponies aren't."

Lulu noticed that Anna's cheeks were red. That was a sure sign that she was angry. "What's the great part, Pam?" Lulu quickly asked.

"The great part," said Pam, "is that Eleanor gave me Starfire. Starfire is my horse now."

Anna jumped to her feet. "You're going to have a *horse*," she said. "You're giving up Lightning!"

"I'm not giving her up," protested Pam. "I'm just not going to ride her all the time. My mother's going to use her for a school pony."

"If you have Starfire, you won't ride her *at all*," shouted Anna. She pulled down Acorn's stirrups. "You're *disloyal* and you're bad Pony Pals." She glared at Pam and Lulu. "Both of you."

"But Anna, I — " Lulu started to say.

"You were ready to move to Africa!" said Anna as she mounted Acorn. "To leave Snow White . . . and us! Well, I'm not giving up my pony."

She turned Acorn around and rode off.

Lulu and Pam looked at each other. What was happening to the Pony Pals?

"Dearest Lulu"

Pam stood up. "Should we follow Anna?" she asked.

"Sometimes it's better to leave her alone for a few minutes," observed Lulu.

"So she can cool down," added Pam as she sat back on the rock.

"It's great that Eleanor gave you Starfire," said Lulu softly.

"Thanks," answered Pam. "I wish it hadn't made Anna mad. And I wish I wasn't too big for Lightning."

"Me, too," said Lulu.

"Anna *is* getting too big for Acorn," said Pam.

"I know," Lulu agreed. "I'll tell her I agree with you. But she isn't going to like it."

Pam stood up again. "Let's go find her."

They walked toward their ponies.

"Do you think she went home?" asked Pam.

"Maybe," answered Lulu. "We'll look for clues to see which way she went."

The girls led their ponies back to the trail. Lulu looked in both directions. She was the best detective of all the Pony Pals.

"We have to figure out if Anna went back the way we came," she said. "Or if she went west."

Pam pointed toward the trail going west. "Look," she said. "Pony plop."

Lulu went over to look at the plop. "It's fresh," she observed. "And here are some hoofprints. Small ones."

Pam and Lulu mounted their ponies and followed Acorn's tracks.

Anna was already way ahead of them on

the trail. As Anna and Acorn passed Ms. Wiggins's field and paddock, Acorn stopped. Ms. Wiggins's horse, Picasso, and her pony, Beauty, were grazing in the field. Anna wanted to keep going. She was mad at Pam and Lulu and wanted to get as far away from them as possible. But Acorn wanted to visit Picasso and Beauty. He whinnied a hello.

Picasso looked up and then went back to grazing. But when Beauty saw Acorn, she whinnied happily and ran up to the fence. Acorn and Anna met her there, and Anna dismounted. The two ponies sniffed each other's noses.

"Pam doesn't care about Lightning anymore," Anna told Beauty and Acorn. "She doesn't care about the Pony Pals."

Beauty nodded as if she understood.

Anna remembered how Pam had found Beauty abandoned in a field. The Pony Pals had saved Beauty's life and convinced Ms. Wiggins to buy her. That was after Ms. Wiggins's old pony, Winston, had died.

"Ms. Wiggins had Winston since she was a

little kid," Anna told the ponies. "She never gave him away. He was always her pony."

Anna heard Pam's voice in her head. *"But when Ms. Wiggins was too big to ride Winston, she rode a horse."*

Lulu's voice came into her head next. *"It didn't mean she didn't love Winston anymore."*

"I know," Anna whispered.

Anna stopped being angry with her friends. Now she felt sad. She knew that Pam was right. She was too big to ride Acorn. Everything was about to change, and there was nothing she could do about it. She buried her face in Acorn's mane and cried.

When Anna finally looked up, her Pony Pals were riding toward her.

"Anna, are you okay?" asked Lulu as she dismounted.

Pam jumped off Lightning. "I'm sorry I made you angry," she said. She put an arm around Anna's shoulder. "Are you okay?"

"I'm sorry I ran away," said Anna. "I'm not mad anymore. Just sad."

"Everything about the Pony Pals is changing," said Lulu.

"Anna and I are too big for our ponies," Pam said. "Your dad wants you to move."

"We still have to stick together," said Anna.

"Let's go see if my dad wrote back," suggested Lulu.

As the girls rode back to the Crandals', they were lost in their own thoughts.

Pam thought, I know I'll learn a lot from riding Starfire, and I'll have fun riding him. But I won't ever love him as much as I love Lightning.

Acorn is a good carriage pony, thought Anna. But I like riding better. That's what the Pony Pals do.

Pam and Anna have outgrown their ponies, thought Lulu. Even if Dad lets me stay in Wiggins, I'll outgrow Snow White, too. What will we do then? Anna's paddock isn't big enough for two ponies and two horses. It's all so complicated. I wish time would stop. I wish we could be Pony Pals forever.

When the Pony Pals got to the Crandals', they cooled down their ponies, took off their tack, and put them in the paddock.

"Hurry," Anna said, running toward the barn. "Let's check the e-mail."

Lulu and Pam ran to catch up with her.

"Maybe my dad didn't even see my e-mail yet," said Lulu. "He might be on safari doing research."

But Mr. Crandal wasn't on safari. He had read his daughter's e-mail. And he had answered it.

The girls sat around the computer. Lulu read the e-mail out loud.

To: Lulu
From: Dad
Subject: Re: Here I am in Wiggins

Dearest Lulu,

I have lived and worked in many different places. After your mother died, I always took you with me. When you turned ten, I thought you should live in one place for a while. So I brought you to Wiggins to live with your Grandmother Sanders. Now I am going to be living in Botswana for at least two years. This is a wonderful and interesting country. I was very happy when I found that there was a good school in my town. This is perfect, I thought. Lulu and I can live together again.

I know it is hard for you to leave your friends, your pony, and your grandmother. She e-mailed me, too. She said that you wanted to stay in Wiggins and that she would like that. I can understand how she feels. You are a wonderful girl. But I am your father. I don't want to miss any more of your growing up.

It's sad to say good-bye to friends and your pony. But I am sure you can be happy here. Just remember, you and I are family. We belong together.

I love you very much.

See you in a week.

Love,
Dad

Tears filled Lulu's eyes. "I have to move," she said. "My father said."

Anna burst into tears. "It's over," she sobbed. "It's all over. The Pony Pals are breaking up."

"I know," whispered Lulu.

Pam was crying, too. "We have a Pony Pal Problem," she said in a choked voice. "It's the biggest Pony Pal Problem of all."

"Lulu's dad said she *has* to leave," said Anna.

"And I want to live with him," added Lulu softly.

"The problem is," explained Pam, "how are we going to end the Pony Pals?"

"There's another problem," said Lulu. "What should I do with Snow White? We have to solve that one first."

"We have to think of three ideas for *both* of these problems," said Pam.

Anna and Lulu slowly rode home along Pony Pal Trail.

How many more times will Snow White

and I ride on this trail? wondered Lulu.

Anna was trying to think of how to end the Pony Pals. But the only thought in her head was that she wanted to be a Pony Pal *forever*.

As they approached a turn in the trail, Acorn lifted his head and neighed a warning.

Tommy Rand sped around the turn on his mountain bike. When he saw Acorn, Tommy skidded to a stop.

Snow White backed up fearfully.

Anna pulled Acorn over to the side of the trail. "Hey!" she shouted at Tommy. "Watch where you're going."

"You watch where *you're* going, Pony Pest," Tommy shouted back.

Meanwhile, Lulu walked Snow White in a circle to calm her down.

Mike and Charlie were right behind Tommy. They stopped their bikes next to his.

"Sorry we scared the ponies," said Mike.

"You didn't do anything," Anna told him. "It was Tommy."

Charlie leaned his bike on a tree and walked over to Snow White. "Hi, Snow White," he said. "I haven't seen you in a long time."

Charlie had ridden Snow White and done western tricks on her. He had even taught Lulu to do some tricks. Maybe Snow White should move out west with Charlie, thought Lulu. He'd take excellent care of her. Tears sprung to Lulu's eyes.

Mike noticed. "What's wrong?" he asked.

"Lulu has to move to Africa," answered Anna. "She's going to live there with her dad."

"You're moving!" said Mike, surprised. "That's awful. What about the Pony Pals?"

"Africa is so far away," added Charlie.

"Good riddance," said Tommy. "We have too many Pony Pests around here. We need pest control." He imitated an exterminator pumping a spray can and laughed his mean laugh.

Mike swung toward him. "Stop it!" he shouted. "Stop being mean. It's not funny."

Anna and Lulu exchanged a glance. They'd never, ever seen Mike stand up to Tommy. Tommy was surprised, too. But only for a second.

"Good riddance to you, too," Tommy spat out at Mike. "You're a bigger pest than they are." He jumped on his bike and rode away.

For the first time ever, Mike didn't go after Tommy.

"He makes me so mad sometimes," mumbled Mike. "He's a lousy friend."

"That's for sure," agreed Lulu.

Charlie patted Mike on the back. "You can find better guys than him to hang out with," he said.

Mike looked at him gratefully and smiled. "I guess," he agreed.

Anna and Lulu dismounted. They led their ponies the rest of the way home. Mike and Charlie walked with them, pushing their bikes.

Lulu told them all about why she had to

move to Africa. Charlie had a lot of questions about riding elephants.

Anna told them about Pam and Starfire. But she didn't tell them that she was getting too big to ride Acorn. There were already too many things to tell.

8

Six Ideas

The next morning, Anna and Lulu rode their ponies to the diner. Lightning was already tied to the hitching post.

When Anna and Lulu went inside, Pam was waiting for them in their favorite booth. The three friends hugged.

"Let's eat before we have our meeting," suggested Pam.

"It'll be easier to concentrate," agreed Lulu.

They had their favorite breakfast — blueberry pancakes. When they'd finished eating, the girls cleared the table. It was time to share their ideas.

"Who wants to go first?" asked Pam.

"I do," answered Lulu. She pulled a piece of paper out of her pocket and read her idea out loud.

Problem #1: I want to give Snow White to Anna. Anna can have two ponies.

Problem #2: We should e-mail one another every week.

"That was my idea about what to do with Snow White," said Pam, smiling.

"Rosalie can always ride Acorn," said Lulu. "She'd love that."

"If I ever had another pony, I would want it to be Snow White," said Anna. "I love Snow White."

"Snow White is a lot taller than Acorn," observed Pam. "You'll be able to ride her for a long time, Anna."

"It won't be so hard to leave Snow White if she's with you," added Lulu.

"Snow White will be here when you come home for vacations," pointed out Anna. "She'll always be your pony."

"And Acorn will still be your pony," concluded Lulu.

Anna tied her drinking straw into a knot. "There's just one problem with our idea," she said. "My mom and dad might not let me take care of two ponies. They're always worrying about my schoolwork."

Lulu remembered once when Anna got failing grades in school. Her parents told her that she couldn't keep Acorn. They'd said that taking care of a pony took up too much of Anna's time. It was one of the first problems the Pony Pals had to solve.

"Should I ask my mom now?" wondered Anna.

Pam looked around for Mrs. Harley. She was busy serving breakfast and running the cash register. "Ask her when she isn't so busy," she suggested. Pam opened her notebook and handed it to Lulu. "Here's my idea for ending the Pony Pals."

Lulu read Pam's idea out loud.

We should make a big scrapbook about being Pony Pals. Lulu can take it with her to Africa.

"That's a great idea," said Lulu. "I have a lot of pictures to put in it."

"Pam, you can write in the scrapbook. You have the best handwriting."

"And you'll draw pictures, Anna," added Lulu. "We can work on it today."

"Don't forget we're going over to Mr. Olson's to see Charlie this morning," Pam reminded Lulu and Anna. "Mike and Rosalie will be there."

"I hope Tommy doesn't show up," said Lulu. "He's the only person in Wiggins I won't miss when I move to Botswana."

"I can't believe that Mike stood up to Tommy yesterday," said Pam.

"Mike didn't apologize for yelling at him or

follow him or anything," added Anna. "That's a first."

Pam looked at Anna. "We forgot all about your idea for the end of the Pony Pals," she said. "What is it?"

"Show us," added Lulu.

Anna opened her sketchbook and put it in the middle of the table. The three friends looked at it together.

Pony Pals 4-Ever ♥

"That's beautiful," exclaimed Pam. "I like how you drew us all connected."

"We should put this drawing in the scrapbook," said Lulu. She smiled at her two best friends. "We'll always be the Pony Pals."

"Pony Pals forever," added Pam.

"But it won't be the same," said Anna as she untied the knot in her straw.

"Nothing stays the same," said Pam sadly. "That's life."

"I wish it wasn't true," said Anna.

"Me, too," agreed Lulu and Pam.

Lulu noticed that Mrs. Harley was coming over to their table. Pam and Anna saw her, too. They all said hello.

"I heard you're moving to Africa, Lulu," Mrs. Harley said. "I'm going to miss you."

"I'll miss you," said Lulu.

Anna's mother put a hand on Lulu's shoulder. "I know you'll miss Snow White, too. I suppose you'll be selling her," she said. "I'm sure Mr. Olson will find her a good home."

The Pony Pals exchanged a glance. This was the time to tell Mrs. Harley their idea.

"Lulu doesn't want to sell Snow White," Anna blurted out.

"I want to give her to Anna," said Lulu.

"Anna's getting too big for Acorn," explained Pam.

"But I want to keep him, too," Anna quickly added. "I can take care of two ponies."

"Anna, you are much too busy with schoolwork to have two ponies," said her mother. "When Lulu leaves, we'll go back to having one pony in the paddock. I don't even know if you can handle that. Lulu does more work with those ponies than you do."

"That's because I have tutoring after school," argued Anna.

"Which you will still have when Lulu's gone," said her mother.

"Acorn and Snow White shouldn't be separated," wailed Anna. "They're best friends. They're stablemates."

"Of course they can be separated," insisted her mother. "Ponies are bought and sold all the time." She sighed. "You can only have one pony. That's more than most kids have. I'm sorry, Anna. You'll have to decide which pony you want."

I Promise

Five customers came into the diner, and Mrs. Harley went to greet them.

"How can I choose between Snow White and Acorn?" Anna cried to her friends. "If I keep Snow White, I'll lose Acorn. If I keep Acorn, Lulu will have to sell Snow White, and I won't have a pony to ride."

"Another Pony Pal Problem!" exclaimed Lulu.

"Charlie and Mike can help us," said Pam.

Anna didn't say anything. Maybe her

mother was right. Maybe she didn't have time to take care of two ponies.

As the girls rode up Mr. Olson's driveway, they saw Charlie and Mike sitting on the riding ring fence. Rosalie was playing with one of the barn cats. The boys waved and Rosalie ran to meet the Pony Pals.

"Can I ride Acorn?" she begged Anna. "Can I, please? Can I?"

"Let her ride while we talk to Mike and Charlie," suggested Lulu.

Lulu and Pam tied their ponies to the hitching post. Anna walked into the riding ring with Rosalie and Acorn.

The Pony Pals sat on the fence with the boys and watched Rosalie ride.

"Did you decide what to do with Snow White?" Charlie asked Lulu. "My uncle said he could get you a good price for her."

"I'm not going to sell her," Lulu told Charlie and Mike. "I want to give her to Anna."

"Snow White is the perfect size for you, Anna," said Charlie.

81

"I want to keep Acorn, too," added Anna.

"If you ride Snow White, maybe Rosalie could ride Acorn more," suggested Mike.

"That's what we thought," said Pam.

"There's just one problem with that idea," Lulu explained. "Anna's mother said she can't have two ponies. She said that it's too much work."

"I can help take care of Snow White and Acorn," offered Mike. He smiled at Anna. "It would be a way for us to pay for Rosalie's riding time."

"You'd do that?" asked Anna, surprised. "Every day?"

"Sure," he answered. "I like ponies."

Mike would never say that if Tommy were here, thought Pam.

Lulu remembered when Mike was afraid of ponies. Even Snow White. Working for Ms. Wiggins had taught him a lot.

Pam and Anna exchanged a glance.

Mike could be a big help, thought Anna. But will my mother agree?

"Do you think your mother will agree to this plan?" Pam asked Anna.

Anna loved it when the Pony Pals were thinking the same thing at the same time. "I don't know," she answered.

"You should write up a contract," Charlie told Mike. "List all the things you'll do to help. You can give the signed contract to Anna's mother."

"That's a *great* idea," said Pam.

"It will show her that you're serious, Mike," added Lulu.

"Would you do that?" asked Anna.

"Sure," agreed Mike.

Rosalie rode over to the fence. A big grin spread across her face.

Acorn looked happy, too. It's better for Acorn to have a shorter rider, thought Anna.

"I love riding more than anything in the whole wide world," Rosalie said.

"Me, too," agreed the Pony Pals and Charlie in unison. They looked at one another and smiled.

"Can I keep riding, Anna?" Rosalie asked.

"Sure," agreed Anna. "Acorn has lots of energy today."

"Rosalie is a really good rider," Pam told Mike. "She has natural talent."

Mike jumped down from the fence. "Let's write the contract now," he said. "I want Rosalie to ride lots."

Lulu stayed outside and watched Rosalie and Acorn. Everyone else went inside the house to work on the contract.

A week from now I'll be back in Africa, thought Lulu. She was sad about leaving her friends and pony. But she knew in her heart that her father was right. They were family. They should live together. Lulu only hoped that Snow White could stay with Anna and Acorn.

After a while, the others came back out. Charlie handed Lulu a paper. "You're supposed to sign the contract," he said. "We're all witnesses."

Lulu read the contract carefully before signing it.

I, Mike Lacey, do hereby agree to take care of the two ponies residing in the Harley paddock. Their names are Acorn (Harley) and Snow White (Sanders).

Here is what I will do every day:

> Fill water buckets
>
> Put out hay and grain

Here is what I will do every other day:

> Clean shed

Here is what I will do once a week:

> Groom Acorn and Snow White
>
> Clean the paddock

Anna Harley will also take care of the ponies and the paddock. But I, Mike Lacey, will do more than Anna does.

I have taken care of a horse and pony at the property of Ms. Wilhelmina Wiggins. She is my reference.

In exchange for taking care of Acorn and Snow White, my sister, Rosalie Lacey, will ride Acorn three times a week.

I promise to do the work.

Signed,

Michael John Lacey

Michael John Lacey

Witnesses:

Anna Marie Harley

Anna Marie Harley

Charles K Johnson

Charles K. Johnson

Pamela Eleanor Crandal

Pamela Eleanor Crandal

Lucinda Sanders

"It's perfect," said Lulu as she added her signature to the contract. She looked at Pam. "I didn't know you had a middle name. Are you named after Eleanor?"

Pam nodded. "Mom and Eleanor rode together all the time when they were younger. They've always been best friends."

"They're still best friends," added Lulu, "even though Eleanor doesn't live in Wiggins and travels all over the world for riding."

"Just like you guys will always be friends," said Charlie.

The Pony Pals exchanged a glance. They knew that Charlie was right. They would always be best friends.

"Should we go back to the diner now and talk to my mom?" asked Anna.

"We should ask her when she's not busy," Lulu observed.

"I think you should ask your father, too," added Pam. "At the same time."

"Let's go to your house and work on the scrapbook," suggested Lulu. "Then when your parents come home, we can talk to them."

"I have to take care of Starfire first," said Pam. "I'll come over as soon as I finish. I'll bring some photos for the scrapbook."

"We can have dinner at my house," said Anna. "My parents are usually in a good mood during dinner."

"Then we can have a sleepover at my house," said Lulu.

"And work on the scrapbook," concluded Pam.

Anna and Lulu spent the afternoon in Anna's bedroom working on the scrapbook. Pam joined them at 4:00.

When Mr. and Mrs. Harley came home at 6:30, the table was set, there was a big salad in the middle of the table, and potatoes were roasting in the oven.

"Nice job, girls," Mrs. Harley said. "Thank you." She handed Anna a bag of baked chicken pieces from the diner.

Anna put the chicken on a platter, and Lulu took the potatoes out of the oven.

When they sat down to dinner, Mr. Harley turned to Lulu. "I heard you're moving to Africa," he said. "It's a wonderful opportunity for you."

"I know," said Lulu. She exchanged a glance with Anna and Pam. Was this the time to talk about Mike and the contract? Anna and Pam nodded.

"I want to give Snow White to Anna," Lulu announced.

"So I've heard," said Mr. Harley. "That's very generous of you." He handed Anna the salad bowl. "Anna, you've really shot up this year. It doesn't surprise me that you outgrew Acorn."

"Rosalie Lacey wants to ride Acorn," said Anna. "He's the perfect size for her."

"The Laceys live in an apartment," said Mrs. Harley. "They don't have a place to keep Acorn. Besides, her mother is *very* anti-pet. Am I right?"

"Very," agreed Lulu.

"That's why I have to keep Acorn here," said Anna. "Rosalie is a wonderful rider, and she loves Acorn."

"Her brother, Mike, loves ponies, too," added Pam.

Lulu handed Mr. Harley the butter. "Mike's a nice guy," she said.

"I thought you girls didn't like Mike and Tommy," said Mr. Harley. "Don't they call you the Pony Pests?"

The girls explained that Tommy was a bad influence on Mike.

"But Mike doesn't hang out with Tommy anymore," concluded Lulu.

"Mike works for Ms. Wiggins," explained Pam. "So he knows a lot about taking care of horses and ponies."

Anna held up the contract. "Actually," she said, "Mike wants to help take care of Snow White and Acorn."

Anna's parents exchanged a look.

"So the ponies won't be separated," explained Lulu.

"And Anna will have plenty of time for tutoring and homework," added Pam.

"Mike wrote down what he would do," said Anna as she handed her mother the contract.

Mrs. Harley silently read the page, then handed it to her husband to read. Except for the ticking of the clock and the hum of the refrigerator, the room was silent.

Mr. and Mrs. Harley exchanged a glance.

"We could try it," said Mr. Harley thoughtfully. "Do you agree?"

Mrs. Harley nodded.

The Pony Pals jumped up from the table and hugged.

The kitchen was no longer silent.

Good-bye, Pony Pals

The next morning, the Pony Pals went to the diner for breakfast. They had blueberry pancakes and looked through the scrapbook.

"I love it," said Anna. "I wish I could have one exactly like it."

"Me, too," agreed Pam.

"Let's ask Mrs. Baxter to make two copies," suggested Lulu. "She has a very fancy copy machine."

Mrs. Baxter was a friend of the Pony Pals. She and her husband ran a real estate agency that was right next to the diner. The

Baxters had owned Snow White before Lulu did, and Mrs. Baxter was always happy to see the Pony Pals.

"What's up, girls?" she asked cheerfully when they walked in.

Lulu explained that she was moving to Africa to be with her father.

Mrs. Baxter wanted to hear all about Lulu's move.

"That sounds wonderful," Mrs. Baxter said. "But I know you are going to miss your Pony Pals and Snow White. Are you going to sell her?"

"I'm giving Snow White to Anna," Lulu explained. "Acorn is too small for her."

"That way Snow White doesn't have to move," said Mrs. Baxter. "Clever girls." She smiled at Lulu. "You've taken wonderful care of Snow White." She turned to Anna. "And I know you will, too."

"We all made a Pony Pal scrapbook for Lulu to take to Africa," said Pam.

"This is it," said Lulu as she handed the scrapbook to Mrs. Baxter.

Mrs. Baxter looked through it. "It's wonderful!" she exclaimed. She pointed to a photo. "Look at this cute picture of Snow White."

"Pam and I want to have our own scrapbooks, too," said Anna. "We wondered if we could use your machine to make color copies."

"I'd be very happy to make copies for you," Mrs. Baxter said enthusiastically.

"We can pay for it," said Pam.

Mrs. Baxter was already at the copy machine. "But I won't let you," she said. "It will be my present to the Pony Pals."

Lulu's last three days in Wiggins were very busy.

Pam and Anna helped her pack her clothes, some of her books and CDs, and her favorite stuffed animals.

Lulu also rode around Wiggins to say good-bye to her favorite people. Anna and Pam went with her. They wanted to spend as much time with Lulu as possible before she left.

The three girls stopped to see Mr. Remington at the library; Ms. McGee at the Historical Society; Mike's grandmother at Good View Nursing Home; Ms. Raskins at St. Francis Animal Shelter; Eve Greeley and her pony, Lucky; Mr. and Mrs. Quinn and their pony, Ginger; Mimi Klein, her parents, and their little pony, Tongo; and Mr. Olson. Everyone Lulu visited said that they were sad to see Lulu go, but were happy that she would be with her father.

The Pony Pals had sleepovers every night.

The first night they were at Anna's.

The second night they were back at Lulu's.

They did everything together. Except one thing. Lulu spent at least an hour both nights alone with Snow White.

On Lulu's last afternoon in Wiggins, the Pony Pals went on one last trail ride and picnic. They rode all over Ms. Wiggins's trails and had a picnic at their favorite spot on Badd Brook.

That night, Dr. and Mrs. Crandal made Lulu a special dinner and invited Grandmother Sanders, Mr. and Mrs. Harley, and Ms. Wiggins. Mrs. Crandal made one of Lulu's all-time favorite meals — spaghetti with meatballs and garlic bread. Ms. Wiggins made a salad of fresh vegetables from her garden. Mrs. Harley brought brownies for dessert. The Crandal twins, Jack and Jill, insisted on sitting on either side of Lulu. It was a fun dinner party, especially when Jack and Jill got them all telling knock-knock jokes. Lulu was surprised that her grandmother knew so many. Anna's father told a bunch of lightbulb jokes, which Anna didn't think were very funny.

Before the Pony Pals had their last barn sleepover, they went to the paddock to say good night to their ponies. Snow White's coat glowed in the light of a big half-moon. The girls stood with their ponies in the center of the paddock and looked up at the moon and twinkling stars.

"Whenever I look at the moon, I will think of you," Lulu told her two best friends.

Anna held Lulu's hand. "I'll think of you

whenever I look at the moon, too," she said.

Pam took Lulu's other hand. "Me, three," she added.

Snow White lowered her head into the middle of the circle they'd made and nickered softly.

After the Pony Pals said good night to their ponies, they went up to the hayloft and crawled into their sleeping bags. They talked late into the night until, one by one, they dropped off to sleep.

Early the next morning, the girls rode to Lulu's. Dew was still on the ground. Lulu breathed in the smell of the early morning air and listened to the chirping birds and the thump of ponies' hooves on the hard-packed trail. Pony Pal Trail wound through the woods ahead of her. Today I'm flying to Africa, she thought.

Charlie, Mike, and Rosalie were waiting for the Pony Pals at the end of the trail.

Rosalie opened the paddock gate for the riders.

"We came to say good-bye," announced Charlie.

The Pony Pals rode into the paddock and dismounted.

Lulu thought Rosalie would run right over to Acorn. But she didn't. She threw her arms around Lulu. "I'm going to miss you," she cried.

Tears sprang to Lulu's eyes. She patted the younger girl's head. "I'm going to miss you, too, Rosalie," she said. "Don't forget, I'll be back to visit." Lulu thought she saw tears in Mike's eyes, too. But she wasn't sure.

"We have a present for you," Rosalie said when their hug ended. Mike handed Lulu a box of candy. "It's for the airplane ride," he explained.

Charlie gave her a red cowboy bandanna. "Wear it when you ride an elephant," he said. "And send me a picture."

"I will," promised Lulu.

Lulu's grandmother came out. "You have to shower and put on clean clothes now," she said.

Half an hour later, Lulu was dressed for her trip. The three girls and Grandmother Sanders took Lulu's luggage out to the porch. Everything was ready.

"I'll get the car from the garage and drive around," said Grandmother.

A lump rose in Lulu's throat. "It's time to say good-bye to Snow White," she said.

Pam and Anna exchanged a glance. They knew that Lulu would want to be alone with her pony when she said good-bye.

"We'll put your suitcases in the car," Pam said.

When Lulu went into the paddock, all three ponies looked up, but only Snow White ran to meet her. Lulu leaned her face against her pony's cheek. "Anna and Mike will take very good care of you," she said. "But I'll miss you and miss you and miss you. You are my most wonderful pony. You always will be."

Snow White nodded her head as if to agree. Lulu hugged her.

A horn honked. "I have to go," she told Snow White.

As Lulu walked away from the paddock, Pam and Anna ran to meet her. The three friends walked arm in arm to the front of Mrs. Sanders's house.

Grandmother Sanders stood by the car holding three little blue boxes in her hand. She gave one to each of the girls.

"Thank you," the Pony Pals said in unison. They grinned at one another.

"Open them together," Grandmother instructed.

The girls opened the boxes and saw identical silver necklaces. Each one had three pony head charms.

"They're memory necklaces so you'll always remember being Pony Pals," explained Grandmother Sanders.

"We're going to be Pony Pals forever," said Anna as she hooked her necklace around Pam's neck.

Pam put her necklace around Lulu's neck. "And best friends," she said.

"A circle of friends," added Lulu as she put her necklace on Anna.

Grandmother Sanders was in the car and had started the motor. "It's time to leave, Lulu," she announced through the open window.

Lulu went around to the other side of the car and got in.

As the car pulled away, she waved to Anna and Pam. They waved back.

But they didn't say good-bye.

THE PONY PALS 4-EVER SCRAPBOOK

STATS ON GIRLS
LULU
Hair Color: Brown
Height: 5 feet
Age: 10 years

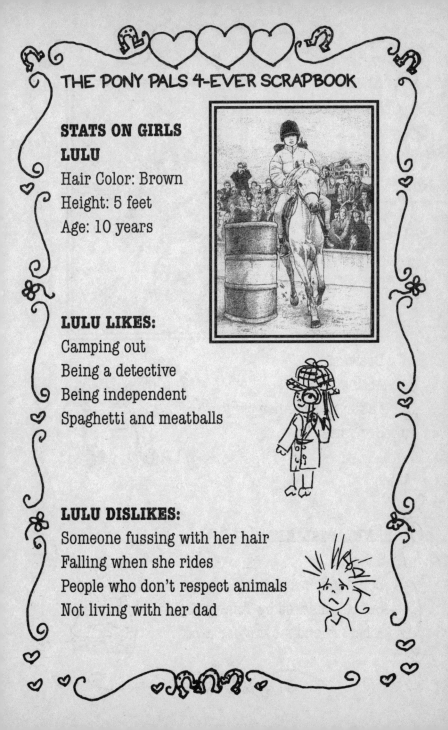

LULU LIKES:
Camping out
Being a detective
Being independent
Spaghetti and meatballs

LULU DISLIKES:
Someone fussing with her hair
Falling when she rides
People who don't respect animals
Not living with her dad

ANNA

Hair Color: Blond
Height: 4 feet
10 inches
Age: 10 years

ANNA LIKES:

Drawing
Acting
Taking care of her pony
Brownies

ANNA DISLIKES:

School
Being indoors
Being mimicked by Tommy Rand
A best friend moving far away

PAM

Hair Color: Black
Height: 5 feet 4 inches
Age: 10 years

PAM LIKES:

School
Taking care of animals
Jumping
Being in charge

PAM DISLIKES:

Horse competitions
Bossy people
Runny eggs
A best friend moving far away

STATS ON PONIES
SNOW WHITE
Breed: Welsh pony
Color: White
Height: 13.2 hands high (54 inches)
Age: 8 years

SNOW WHITE LIKES:
Human company
Apples
Jumping
Cold weather

SNOW WHITE DISLIKES:
Barbed wire
Flies
Unkind shouting
Being alone

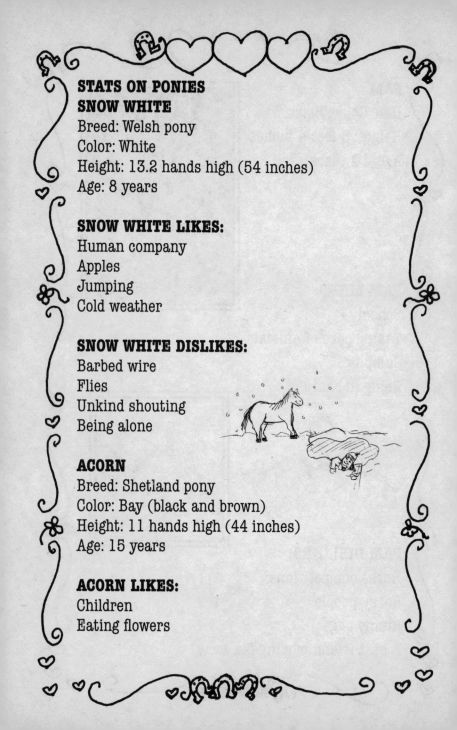

ACORN
Breed: Shetland pony
Color: Bay (black and brown)
Height: 11 hands high (44 inches)
Age: 15 years

ACORN LIKES:
Children
Eating flowers

Pony Pal Trail
Jumping

ACORN DISLIKES:
Being told what to do
Hot weather
Moving from home to home
Tommy Rand

LIGHTNING
Breed: Connemara pony
Color: Chestnut
Height: 14 hands high (56 inches)
Age: 10 years

LIGHTNING LIKES:
Pony Pals
Woolie
Being in horse shows
Apples

LIGHTNING DISLIKES:
Being sick
Getting shots
Sleeping indoors
Too many apples

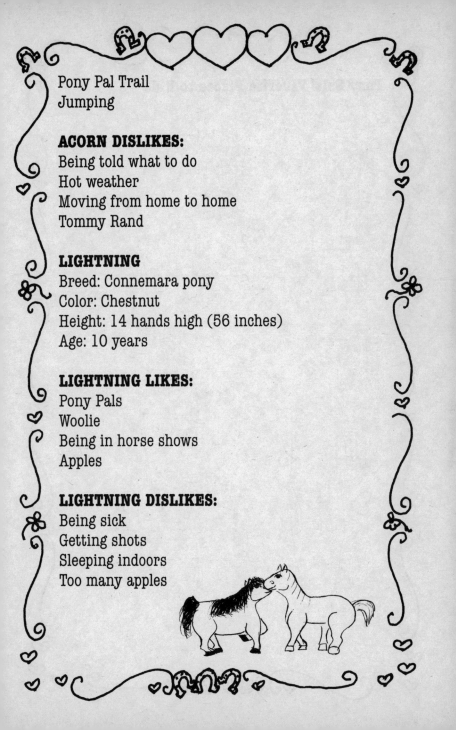

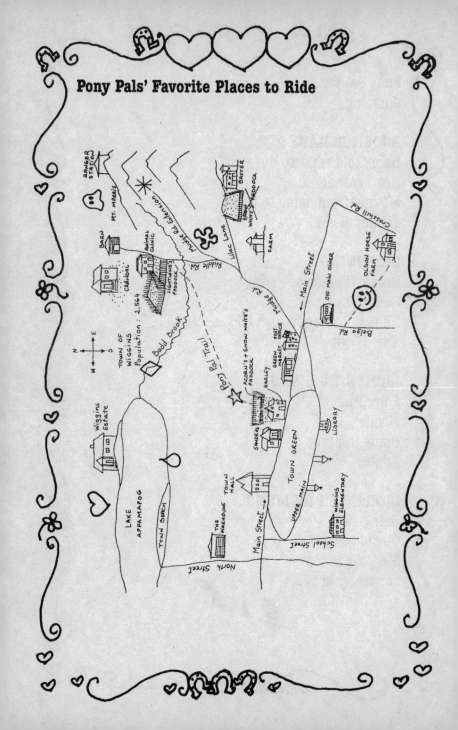

MAP KEY:

☆ Pony Pal Trail

◇ Along Badd Brook

♡ Ms. Wiggins's Trails

✳ Mudge Road Extension

👻 In Morristown — A real ghost town

🍀 Lilac Lane

💧 Around Lake Appamapog

☺ Trail to Olson Farm from Belgo Road

Pony Pals' Favorite Foods at Off-Main Diner

Brownies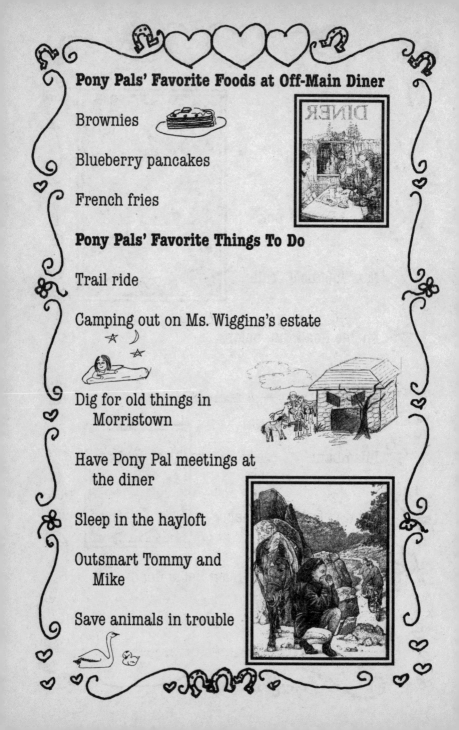

Blueberry pancakes

French fries

Pony Pals' Favorite Things To Do

Trail ride

Camping out on Ms. Wiggins's estate

Dig for old things in
Morristown

Have Pony Pal meetings at
the diner

Sleep in the hayloft

Outsmart Tommy and
Mike

Save animals in trouble

The Happiest Pony Pal Moment

When Lulu got Snow White and we knew we would be the Pony Pals

The Saddest Pony Pal Moment

When we found out that Lulu was moving

Pony Pal Promises
Pam

I will always love Lightning and give
her attention.
I will take excellent care of Starfire.
I will go on lots of trail rides with Starfire,
Anna, and Snow White.
I will e-mail Lulu at least once a week.
I will be a Pony Pal 4-Ever.

Pamela Eleanor Crandal

Anna

I will take excellent care of Acorn
and Snow White.
Snow White and I will go on trail rides
with Pam and Starfire.
I will take Rosalie and Acorn on trail rides.
I will work hard at school and do my
homework so I can keep Acorn and Snow White.
I will e-mail Lulu at least once a week and
tell her all about Snow White.
I will be a Pony Pal 4-Ever.

Anna Marie Harley

Lulu

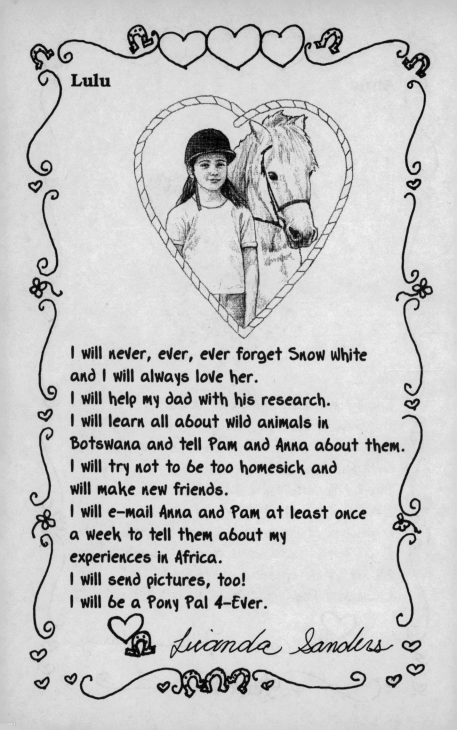

I will never, ever, ever forget Snow White
and I will always love her.
I will help my dad with his research.
I will learn all about wild animals in
Botswana and tell Pam and Anna about them.
I will try not to be too homesick and
will make new friends.
I will e-mail Anna and Pam at least once
a week to tell them about my
experiences in Africa.
I will send pictures, too!
I will be a Pony Pal 4-Ever.

Lucinda Sanders

Dear Pony Pal,

THE LAST PONY RIDE is the last Pony Pal book. I will miss the girls, their ponies, neighbors, and animal friends. I might even miss Tommy Rand.

Pam, Anna, and Lulu are strong, smart, independent, and kind. They also have a lot of fun with their ponies and one another. But, like real girls, the Pony Pals face problems in their lives. In each one of the forty-three Pony Pal books, the girls have had a problem or mystery to solve.

The biggest problems the Pony Pals face are in this Super Special. Pam and Anna have outgrown their ponies and Lulu has to move away and decide what to do with Snow White. In the end, the three best friends promise to be Pony Pals 4-ever.

After so many stories, the Pony Pals and their adventures are part of me. I will always remember them. I am a Pony Pal 4-ever. I hope you are, too.

These stories have all been for you, Pony Pal Readers.

Jeanne Betancourt

P.S. Look for my new series, Three Girls in the City.